D1824935

BLACK DEATH

(LONE WOLVES 2)

AARON SOLOMON

PublishAmerica
Baltimore

Softcover 9781627099509
PUBLISHED BY PUBLISHAMERICA, LLLP
www.publishamerica.com
Baltimore

Printed in the United States of America

PROLOGUE

I came to in someone else's bed, memories of my past still racking my brain. "Shh. He's waking up." Said a voice as I slowly opened my eyes to see the figure of yet another wolf standing over me. Her fur was a lovely golden brown and she had bangs completely covering her right eye. She lifted it up and I knew who she was almost instantly. "Lilly?" I asked curiously. She smiled. "Ah, you remember me brother, after all these years." Lilly was indeed my long lost younger sister who I had not seen since the last 23 years ago when we were pups growing up in the Alaskan wilderness. After I was adopted by humans, she went her own way and studied to become a veterinarian at Alaska State University and eventually moved to Maryland where she started her career at Howard County General Hospital in mine and my human's hometown of Columbia. I sat up to embrace her in a tight lock hug but soon regretted it, feeling a sharp pain in my abdomen. Whoa. Save the pup love for later big bro. Right now, we need to get you fully healed." She said. "For now, just take your time and get some rest." And with that, I slowly closed my eyes and drifted off into sleep while Lilly continued to use her gift of healing.

1

Soon enough, three days later, my time came and I finally made a full recovery. Kari Voucher had decided to move in with me and became my dearest friend and caretaker in all the days since the Steele incident. Even as much as we both yearned to marry, we couldn't because of a corrupt government who passed a law saying that "all canines were equal" and could not interact romantically with felines or "individuals of the opposite species." So, we had no choice but to keep our love "locked down." Not too long after my recovery, I soon return to my position at the DEA to lead these men, my brothers, with honor just as my father did years before me. At 6:40 in the morning, I'm already up and at em to start the old grime all over again. After a quick wash up in the restroom, I paused and soon found myself staring at a disfigured reflection of my face in the pristine mirror. My once amber left eye was now a lighter gold color topped off with a long jagged scar starting from the top of the eyelid and ending at the bottom. I looked like something out of "The Lion King" in wolf form. "Just then, my newlywed Kari called in. "Hurry honey! Or you'll be late for your first day back!" I straightened up my still ruffled golden red fur and quickly sprang up from the sink and into the bedroom. Slipping on a brown leather jacket and some khakis, I grab my P229 pistol and badge off the dresser and step into my usual polished, black dress boots. After giving Kari a quick nuzzle goodbye, I open the door to be coldly embraced by the mid October air. I open the door to my Infinite and brace myself for the one hell of a drive down to headquarters.

2

I arrived at 7:09 AM, just on the money of my scheduled arrival time of 7:15. Ditching the old gal in the lot, I casually punch in, only to be greeted by a chorus of cheers and applause. Among the crowd, was my proud boss, Lieutenant Tony Atkinson. "Welcome back to the team, Solomon." He said warmly. "It has come to my attention that the Steele case has been successfully brought to a close. It brings me great honor to reward you with this promotion as group supervisor. You have brought peace to your father and yourself" I beamed with pride. "Thank you sir. It is a great honor I will hold dearly." "But..." He went on. "I am going to have to throw you back in the fire right away." "Good enough for me, sir" I replied eagerly. He smiled. "Good. I have always been very fond of your "Can-Do" attitude." He continued on with the briefing. He informed me that the all out drug war was far from over. In fact, it had only spread its way like wildfire further south into Peru. As it turns out, Steele had a son by the name of Zeke Cortez who was the leader of the La Grippe, a newly formed cartel of malevolent and more ruthless coyotes name for the slimy vermin himself. Recent intelligence indicated Cortez's Right hand man and one of our longtime contacts working for the cartel, had been captured and was being held at an abandoned factory after he was caught retrieving documents containing valuable information about a suspicious shipment headed for U.S. soil. Our mission, yank the contact and find these documents in which his head honcho held so sacred. "Consider it done." I said and began to suit up with the rest of my team. Devil Dog was back in business.

3

I rose up from the forest floor. Our newest addition of the group, Noah Hopkins stood motionless leaning against a tree, puffing lightly on a Cuban cigar. He straightened up when he saw me stand. "Hutch, we're just outside the Village" "Copy. I'll pick you up in one hour. You are jumpin into some deep shit Graystripe." Noah chuckled at his Hutch's remark. "I think I can hold my own. Thanks." He replied taking one last drag on his coheeba. His pure solid gray fur glistening in the sunlight for which he was aptly nicknamed. Being the only feline of the group, he seemed to be used to some of the constant pressure from his higher seniority members. "Ok. You heard the man. Let's roll." I said pulling back the charging handle on my newly issued ACR Assault rifle. He picked up his MP5A2 submachine gun and we crept slowly forward into the southeast corner of the village, checking our flanks as we slid by the waiting cartel militia. A last, we reached the target building, three miles up the road. After silently subduing and cuffing the two coyotes at the entrance, Graystripe took point and we move cautiously up the stairs to the balcony. Slipping by two more guards around the corner, we carefully make our way down the corridor and approach the door to the contact's office located on the left. At a count of three, Graystripe kicked it in. The coyotes inside the room raised their XM8 rifles and prepared to fire, only to be taken down with one precisely aimed burst shot from our weapons. Then, revealed a horrific sight. A red and cream wolf sat strapped to a steel chair with arm restraints in the center of the large room. He looked up at me with two bright neon green orbs and I suddenly realized, this was no ordinary Lackey or henchman. This was in fact my brother.

4

"We meet again, brother" Said Garth, still looking up at me from the chair. "After all these years." Garth Myers was indeed my conniving brother who had made a name for himself in the crime industry. Even as a pup, our family tried everything in our power to keep him moving down the right path. It was of no use to Garth. By the time he was 14, he had already dropped out of school and turned his full attention to the streets. At the time, I graduated the training academy, he had already committed every crime in the book, ranging from robbery to Grand theft auto which lead him to change his last name from Solomon to a more cunning character. But I never thought this. Never would I think he would end up working under the rule of the son of the most backstabbing, murderous drug cartel leaders in criminal history. "So, you got your ass in a jam eh, Garth? Why am I not surprised." I snorted. "Just get me out of this deathtrap" He snapped. "Why?" I asked. "So, you can go back to your 'Master'? You're bad luck, Garth. You've robbed every bank from hell to Houston. Why should I trust you? More importantly, why should my agency trust you?" I growled back. "My guys are crossing borders, bro. The goods they're transporting are probably half way across Cuba by now." "He's right boss." Noah cut in. "We've got a job to do. We need to put the past behind us." I sighed deep in thought. "You're right Gray." I said pulling Steele's old knife out of my pocket. Kari had retrieved it from him and gave it to me as a gift and as a token of our love together. Starting with the arm restraints first, I later snipped off the last strap and Garth breathed a sigh of relief. "Thanks man. I knew you'd come to your senses." The minute after his finished his statement, There was an indistinct shout behind us in what sounded like Spanish. "Looks like we got company." He said. Two Mercenaries appeared in the doorway. I could tell they weren't going down without a fight. Before they even had a chance to aim, I raised my ACR and opened fire bringing them both down almost at once. We grabbed Garth and pushed forward through the slum of Coyotes down the stairs and outside of the factory compound. Guns roaring, we finally made our way into the village to the extraction point, taking down a few more cartel members as we went. A minute later, just when we thought we were going to be overrun, a black unmarked van speeds in on scene. The double doors in the back burst open and I hear Hutch's voice yell "Get in!" Without hesitation, one by one, we did just that. Noah slammed the doors behind him as bullets bit like an apple into them. "Step on it!" Hutch barked out and we took off. Garth let out another sigh of relief. "Can't thank you enough, brother." He said gratefully. "What about the documents, Garth?" I asked. "Oh yes." He reached down into his jeans and handed me a tan manila folder. I read it immediately and gasped, wide eyed by the results. "Boys, we got a priority 1 target and it's damn much bigger than we thought." "What is it?" Noah asked rather nervously. "A sub."

5

"In position" Graystripe called out over his helmet mike. "HQ, radio check. Over" I reported. "Devil Dog, copy. You and your team keep your eyes peeled for that vessel. "Roger Wilco" "Just don't start the party without us." Hutch replied. Tuesday, November 13th, we had just gotten called out on a wholly new assignment. Turns out the information Garth had given us turned up a heroine submarine scheduled to hit U.S. Soil at 10.00 A.M. We sat motionless on the bottom of the ocean floor, my clunky armored diving suit feeling like a copper brick as gently I took a knee. Suddenly, a massive object rumbled overhead. As soon as the tail end was clear, we made our move. Tapping the heels of my copper diving boots together, I activate the thrusters and slowly ascend upward toward the sub. I grabbed the wheel of the hatch and turned it as hard as I could. One by one, we clambered down the ladder to the main deck. The Cartel members inside were instantly alerted of our presence. I raised my ACR and fired back, hitting one of them twice in the chest. A last, we fought our way to the cargo hold. Noah immediately got to work planting explosives on the huge crates containing more than 1,000 kilos of "Black Paw" heroine. The minute after he finished, there was an indistinct shout. Guns blazing, we pushed forward and made our way through the slum of coyotes to the escape hatch.

Swimming slowly up to the surface, we watch in satisfaction as the vessel soon was reduced to a pattern of bright red orange flashes. Our mission was officially complete.

6

I returned to Springfield on the morning of the next day. Finally, we caught a break. I decided to give Kari some alone time back at home and swing by Lilly's house down in Columbia of the predominantly fox state of Maryland. The minute I parked my Infinite in the driveway under the carport, here comes Lilly dashing out of the house barefoot like a country wolf and wrapping her arms around me tightly in a bear like hug. "It's more than wonderful to see you again, brother" She said happily. "The same goes to you little sis" I replied. "What are you doing here?" She asked. "Aren't you DEA wolves supposed to be working on Wednesdays?" "That's why the boss gives us a little something called a day off." I said playfully giving her a noogey. She giggled and we stepped inside her warm and picturesque abode. Hours soon passed and at 5:30 in the evening, our time together had come to an end. I grabbed my jacket off the coat hanger and she strolled me out to my car, still burying her face in my shoulder. Before opening the door, I reached into my jean pocket and pulled out the chestnut handled hunting knife with the words "Always faithful" engraved in Spanish on the blade. "Take this" I said. "You've well earned it. Thank you for saving me, sis." She looked thoughtfully at the knife then tucked it away in her belt hoop and said softly "I will always treasure it" I smiled and turned to leave. But before I could get one foot in my car, I hear the engine of a black Cadillac escalade roaring up the street. The familiar stench of trouble filled the air. "Go in the house" I said to Lilly urgently and quickly followed her inside. From my position behind the wall, I could just make out the figures of two coyotes dressed in military camo style uniforms opening the back door for a red furred Dingo slowly walking toward the doorstep. "Oh shit. Get down!" I shouted, knowing instantly who it was. Suddenly, there was a loud bang and the door was now nothing but a pile of broken wood and brass. I grasp for my pistol only to hear a loud pop and be brought down by a tremendous force. "No!" I hear Lilly cry out. "Do you know who I am?" I hear Cortez ask her. "Yes." "Then you know what I want." "You're fucking insane!" Lilly burst out. "My Cartel will claim all jurisdiction of the United States, even if we must tear it down piece by piece. Starting with your own flesh and blood. I want those documents, Mrs. Solomon." "I don't know what you're talking about!" Lilly replied. "Every canine has their weakness." He said. "Seize her." Hearing Lilly's desperate cries, I wait until the convoy is outside before snapping open my eyes and removing a .45 slug from the body armor under my t shirt. I jump to my feet and sprint out into the parking lot just as the Cadillac starts to speed away down the road. I draw my pistol but cannot risk taking the shot. I knew that one missed step could cost my sister's life.

7

I'm dashing home, moving as fast as the limit would allow down the freeway. I knew I had to get back to Garth. He would be my only shot at gathering all possible info on finding his former superior. Fortunately, I didn't have to look far. I found him back at home sitting across from Kari on the Sofa. "Brother what's wrong?" He asked noticing my distraught expression. "Lilly has been compromised." "In English?" "In other words, she was kidnapped. Your boss wants the documents. Tell me where he's taking her. I have to stop him!" I said putting my paws on his shoulders. "Ok. Calm down. I'll tell you everything you need to know." He told me about an abandoned airfield used by the La Grippe for shipments coming into and out of the U.S. located just south of Springfield. "What's security look like?" I asked. "The whole place is basically a fortress on solid ground. You got only one way in or out." "So much for stealth then." I replied. "Wait." Kari said standing up. "Take me with you." "Honey, no. This is too dangerous for—" "Two heads are always better than one" She said. "Especially those with past experience on the outside." I pondered for a moment then agreed to put Garth in charge of communications while Kari and the rest of the team went in. We nuzzled warmly before hunkering down for a day of well needed rest. Lilly would soon be back in our grasps.

8

"Command, window is closing fast. We're ready to kick this off. "Roger Devil Dog. You've got the all clear. Mission is a go."

"Black Friday", October 26, 2021. One day before this daring quest, we had just gotten briefed on our objective to infiltrate a nearby airfield on the southeastern side of Virginia. The fight against the La Grippe and the search for Lilly had all commenced at once. For this mission, We were assigned a new team member, a vixen female agent of the FBI's Hostage Rescue Unit who had natural beauty written all over her. The name was Ashley Phelps, a Colorado native who unlike most She wolves I've known, spent most of her youth sniping elk in the wilderness. "I assure you, she's quite skilled." Atkinson had once said. "No doubt." I quietly agreed. I knew her stunning and innate physical appearance had said much in the eyes of others. Now, it was time to test those skills out in the field against one of the most vindictive canine drug cartels known to society. "Heads up gents. We're here." Noah announced cocking his weapon. I repeated the same process with my ACR and readied up as Hutch punched it through the gate. Almost instantly, the canines behind it began to rain fire down on us. Only odd thing was: these were not at all coyotes. They were gray wolves.

I got on the horn with Garth. "Brother, we're taking fire from our own kind! None of these are Cortez's Kytes. What the hell's goin on?" "Cortez recruits some wolves for his organization out of North America. These canines are not your kind in any way. Put them down. Put them down hard." "Affirmative." I answered feeling a little uneasy. Killing animals of our own family class was one thing, but having to kill animals of our exact species seemed to be way too extreme. Cortez was most indefinitely going to pay. I followed my brother's instruction to the letter and began to fire back at the La Grippe wolves. I gave Graystripe the order to cover us on "overwatch" while Ashley, Hutch, and I move in to search the first hanger. Discovering it empty, we head back out to the runway and prepare to move to the next when..."Help! Help me!!" Lilly's soprano voice cried out in sheer terror from behind me. From my position a few yards away in front of the previous hangar, I could see the infamous Cartel leader, Cortez stuffing my sister at gunpoint into a small Learjet. I brought my ACR up to aim an opted to fire on him, but to my surprise, Graystripe motioned with a paw "Hold fire" and Ashley soon stopped me. "We can't risk it." She said. "We lost her." Just then, a familiar pure white wolf stepped toward the black stretch parked beside the plane. I remembered back to the previous week. Garth had given me info on a particular wolf named Gordon Thomas who was the head of operations of the now North American branch of the La Grippe. "If anyone can tell you where sis is going, it's him." Garth's voice echoed in the back of my mind. "No. Not yet." I replied to Ashley and gathered up the rest of my team into the van. Hutch slammed on the gas and we were instantly in hot pursuit.

9

We chased him on. On through the rural areas of the Countryside and soon leave them behind as we enter the streets of Tappahannock into general population. I made a split second decision to terminate the perilous chase before the civilians were scathed. I carefully aimed down the holographic sight of my ACR and squeezed off six rounds into the grenadier's torso and another 4 into the driver's head and back. The car sideswiped and was soon pinned between our van and a nearby building down in an alley. The back door opened and I could see Thomas stagger out, his pure white fur red with specs of blood, trying to book it. I bolted up from behind and thwarted his attempt to climb a chain link fence. He fell hard to the pavement. I grab his paws and snap on the cuffs. "Devil dog to command: package secure. Aren't you, ya limey bastard." "Bring him in for a little heart to heart. We'll drain any info out of him on Cortez." "Leave that part to me"

10

I established contact with my brother again at the interrogation room back at division in Springfield. "Any luck getting our little friend here to spill his guts?" I asked him. "Oh, they will spill. One way, or another." Garth said almost homicidally. "Kiss my ass, mutt!" Thomas spat. I stepped fourth. "You wanna repeat that, douche bag?" I responded in a hard tone. Just then, his whole expression suddenly changed from arrogant and defensive to petrified and flabbergasted. Grabbing the collar of his scruffy white dress shirt, I slam his head against the stainless steel table and jerk him back to his position in the chair. "Speak, Damn you!" Garth burst out. Thomas looked up nervously, slowly extending a finger toward me. "I know you…Winston's boy, right? The smart one" "What the hell's he talking about? How do you know my father?!" Garth then spoke up. "Aaron, I think it's time I explain something I should've explained a long time ago" He began to take me back to the time when he was in his adolescence, still roaming the streets trying to find at least someone willing to employ a dropout, a truant of society. Then, his luck soon changed. Gordon found him one day and offered to give him some decent odd jobs around the city. Turns out, these jobs were not at all what he bargained for. At the age of only eighteen, Gordon had fully twisted him into something so sick it almost couldn't die. To become a member of his compatriot, Steele's Cartel. But Father was always one step ahead. He knew of Thomas's true intentions from the very beginning. He tried to stop him, only to succeed in being put down by the organization's Overseer, Victor Steele. "You see brother..." Garth continued. "Gordon is the reason I became a La Grippe."

11

I sat down on my bed, still trying to digest the details I had heard just 18 hours ago. Garth was innocent, just a lonely truant forced into an guild of blood thirsty drug dealers, murderers, and savage beasts under the Iron boot of his own kind and my father's main adversary. Just then, through the borage of memories, my father's warm, tranquil voice seemed itself into my head. "Aaron? Aaron...Aaron!" I awoke with a start, only to be warmly greeted by my mate-to-be sitting at the foot of my large double bed. "Hey. Uh, what are you doing up so early hon?" I asked groggily. She chuckled. "It's seven o clock. By the way, your boss called earlier. Said he needs to speak to you right away." She replied, her voice screaming urgency. Still dressed in my "raid gear" from the previous day, I hop in my ride and turn the engine over for the quick drive back down to division. I arrive to find lieutenant Atkinson, Noah and the rest of the team at the briefing room table. "Ah. Man of the hour." Atkinson said on my arrival. He gracefully pulled out an empty chair. "Sit." He said and then jumped straight to the point. "Thanks to your brother, we were able to extract all the Intel we needed from that little 'one on one' with Thomas last night. Speaking of which, you never did tell me you had a Siamese twin." He said, his last comment earning a slight chuckle from Graystripe and a few others.

He continued on to the mission plan. He said that Thomas gave us Intel on an apartment complex run by Cortez and the La Grippe that was once used to cache weapons near Buenos Aires, Argentina. The bread and butter of it all, Lilly was being held there along with a new drug known as "Basalt" out to poison the entire U.S. eastern seaboard. Our mission was plain and simple. Infiltrate the compound to find the Basalt shipment and wipe out any threats that stood in between bringing down the poisoner at his source and the bang that started it all…Bringing home my little sister.

12

We watched our two targets intently from our hiding spot behind a tree a few yards away in the lush Argentine forest. Hey were heavily armed with full 5.56 round AKs and ammunition and military grade fragmentation grenades. "Damn. Those do not look like he silent type." Noah said a little unnerved. "No they don't" I replied looking down the red dot scope of my old M4. I took a breath and squeezed off 5 rounds into the craniums of each of the pair of coyotes. "They are now" I said earning an impressed look from the cat. "Nice one mate" He said and we move further up the narrow path toward the compound. We came upon two more guards near the main gate of the vast array of structures separated by a massive red iron gate. On a three count, we raised our weapons and fired 4 more silenced shots into the coyotes and buddy climbed over the top of the huge Iron Gate. Finally, we approached the first building located just beyond the main entrance. Once in position, I give the go order and we carefully head in, checking our corners to ensure not to break stealth. Declaring it clear, we continue our search, gradually moving upstairs to an empty bedroom. After a thorough sweep, we call it in empty and continue on through the back door back out onto the street. Soon, we approached a pitch black void of an intersection, guarded only by a single vintage style lamppost with a dim, naked bulb. A couple of feet away, like a soldier without an army, sat the target building on a hillside just up the road. With our weapons locked and loaded, we stacked up on the door and were just about to breach it when…"Double D! Graystripe!" Hutch and Ashley were just bounding up the hill from the Northern side of the village just as time planned.

"Gonna start the party without us, eh?" Hutch panted. "Hm, from where I'm standing it looks like you were a little late to it" I teased. "We may have taken a wrong turn or two along the way." He said and held out his paw. "For Winston" we said in unison after clasping paws and he kicked in the door. It was pitch black inside the villa, but we had decided to leave off the m500 flashlights mounted on the side of our rifles as a chance to remain anonymous to any occupants that may have been told of our arrival here. Just across the room, a single beam of light peeked out from under the crack of the door to the next room. I kicked it in and had just stepped inside when a sudden concrete load was released hard on my back. I whirled around to see a La Grippe coyote pointing an AKM machine gun dead at my chest. He uttered something in Spanish but was soon brought down by a clean shot to the head made by none other than Greystripe. "Boss!" He cried rushing to my aid. "I'm okay." I reassured him as he helped me to my feet. "Where'd you learn to shoot like that Gray? Marksmanship's not a quality skill taught at the academy." I said. He beamed. "I have my secrets"

The minute after he said that, three more Spanish voices were heard and coyotes began to flood the entire corridor. "Looks like they won't stay secrets for long" I said grabbing cover behind the wall. Through a borage of bullets, we pushed forward and made our way through the corridor and into the next room. We were surprised with our discovery. In the back corner was an entire lab with huge crates of fresh basalt neatly stacked in an enormous pile. I knew there was no time to confiscate it all. I made a desperate decision that would probably be the end of one if not all the lives of my team. "Gray, plant the explosives. We're goin hot"

13

Once Noah had successfully put the demolitions in place, we carefully wended our way out of the lab around a corner to the door of the next room. We once again stacked up and prepared to enter as it was Greystripe's turn to kick it in. Then, what I saw inside made my heart drop from my chest and into the pit of my stomach. There, sitting dead as a doornail in a pool of blood at a steel table, was my fiancée Kari Voucher. Cortez stood in front of us, holding an m1911 pistol with the word "Maria" engraved into the slide. Lilly sat across from Kari's lifeless body with sheer panic and terror in her blue eyes. Total silence filled the room. Then, at that very moment, Hutch made a quick lunge and in seconds, was on top of Cortez with the two exchanging blows to each other's face. He then paused for a minute and yelled. "Go Aaron! Go now! I'll handle this prick" I took that as my cue and rushed to my sister's aid. Fortunately, she was fine with only a few scratches and bruises that looked as though they'd heal in no time flat. I used Steele's knife to cut the rope bounds and we quickly headed for the exit. Greystripe called it in. "Command this is Delta one six. Package is secure. Request immediate extraction." "Roger rook we're sending a chopper your way. ETA, 10 minutes." "Shit! Nothing takes ten minutes!" I grumbled. A last, we make it outside. I suddenly remembered that Hutch and Cortez were still inside. "Hutch, Get outta-!" Before I could get the last word out, the building was soon reduced into a massive inferno and ash. I couldn't believe it. I had just watched my closest friend die along with his adversary by our own paws. I rushed into the chopper and cuddled with my sister. Her ordeal was finally over.

Would you like to see your manuscript become a book?

If you are interested in becoming a PublishAmerica author, please submit your manuscript for possible publication to us at:

acquisitions@publishamerica.com

You may also mail in your manuscript to:

**PublishAmerica
PO Box 151
Frederick, MD 21705**

We also offer free graphics for Children's Picture Books!

---

www.publishamerica.com

Lightning Source UK Ltd.
Milton Keynes UK
UKOW052216090713

213519UK00001B/51/P